880

5.5

THE STORY OF A SEAGULL AND THE CAT WHO TAUGHT HER TO FLY

BY LUIS SEPÚLVEDA

TRANSLATED FROM THE SPANISH BY

MARGARET SAYERS PEDEN

ILLUSTRATIONS BY

CHRIS SHEBAN

 ARTHUR A. LEVINE BOOKS
AN IMPRINT OF SCHOLASTIC PRESS

For my sons, SEBASTIÁN, MAX, and LEÓN,

the number-one crew for my dreams;

for the port of HAMBURG,

because that's where I went aboard;

and for my cat, ZORBA, of course

Text copyright © 1996 by Luis Sepúlveda • Translation copyright © 2003 by Margaret Sayers Peden • Illustrations copyright © 2003 by Chris Sheban

All rights reserved. Published by Scholastic Press, a division of Scholastic Inc., *Publishers since 1920*, by arrangement with Tusquets Editores, S. A. SCHOLASTIC, SCHOLASTIC PRESS and the LANTERN LOGO are trademarks and/or registered trademarks of Scholastic Inc.

No part of this publication may be reproduced, or stored in a retrieval system, or transmitted in any form or by any means, electronic, mechanical, photocopying, recording, or otherwise, without written permission of the publisher. For information regarding permission, write to Scholastic Inc., Attention: Permissions Department, 557 Broadway, New York, NY 10012.

LIBRARY OF CONGRESS CATALOGING-IN-PUBLICATION DATA

Sepúlveda, Luis, 1949–

[Historia de una gaviota y del gato que le enseñó a volar. English]

The story of a seagull and the cat who taught her to fly / by Luis Sepúlveda; translated by Margaret Sayers Peden; illustrated by Chris Sheban.   p. cm.

Summary: A seagull, dying from the effects of an oil spill, entrusts her egg to Zorba the cat, who promises to care for it until her chick hatches, then teach the chick to fly.

ISBN 0-439-40186-0

[1. Gulls—Fiction. 2. Cats—Fiction. 3. Flight—Fiction. 4. Oil spills—Fiction.] I. Peden, Margaret Sayers. II. Sheban, Chris, ill.   III. Title.   PZ7.S4796 St 2003   [Fic]—dc21   2002152124

10 9 8 7 6 5 4 3 2 1   03 04 05 06 07

First American edition, September 2003   Printed in the United States of America 37

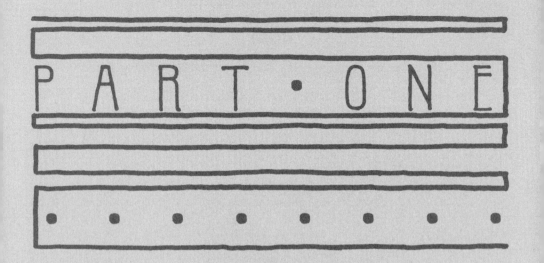

PART · ONE

ONE • THE NORTH SEA

"SCHOOL OF HERRING PORTSIDE!" the lookout gull announced, and the flock from the Red Sand Lighthouse received the news with shrieks of relief.

They had been flying for six hours without a break, and although the pilot gulls had found currents of warm air that made for pleasant gliding above the waves, they needed to renew their strength—and what better for that than a good mess of herring?

They were flying over the mouth of the Elbe River where it flows into the North Sea. From high above they saw ships lining up one after the other like patient and disciplined whales waiting their turn to swim out to open sea. Once there, the flock would get their bearings and spread out toward all the ports of the planet.

Kengah, a female gull with feathers the color of silver, especially liked to observe the ships' flags, for she knew that every one of them represented a way of speaking, of naming the same things with different words.

"Humans really have hard work of it," Kengah had once commented to a fellow she-gull. "Not at all like us gulls, who screech the same the world round."

"You're right. And most amazing of all is that sometimes they manage to understand one another," her gull friend had squawked.

Beyond the shoreline, the landscape turned bright green. Kengah could see an enormous pasture dotted with flocks of sheep grazing under the protection of the dikes and the lazy vanes of the windmills.

Following instructions from the pilot gulls, the flock from Red Sand Lighthouse seized a current of cold air and dived toward the shoal of herrings. One hundred and twenty bodies sliced into the water like arrows, and when they came to the surface each gull had a herring in its bill.

Tasty herring. Tasty and fat. Precisely what they needed to renew their energy before continuing their flight toward Den Helder, where they were to join the flock from the Frisian Islands.

According to their flight plan, they would then fly on to Calais, in the strait of Dover, and on through the English Channel, where they would be met by flocks from the Bay of the Seine and the Gulf of Saint-Malo. Then they would fly together till they reached the skies over the Bay of Biscay.

By then there would be a thousand gulls, a swiftly moving silver cloud that would be enlarged by the addition of flocks from Belle-Île-en-Mer, the Île d'Oléron, Cape Machichaco, Cape Ajo, and Cape Peñas. When all the gulls authorized by the law of the sea and the winds gathered over the Bay of Biscay, the Grand Convention of the Baltic and North Seas and the Atlantic Ocean could begin.

It would be a beautiful time, Kengah thought as she gulped down her third herring. As they did every year, they would listen to interesting stories, especially the ones told by the gulls from Cape Peñas, tireless voyagers who sometimes flew as far as the Canaries or Cape Verde Islands.

Female gulls like her would devote themselves to feasting on sardines and squid, while the males prepared nests at the edge of a cliff. There the female gulls would lay their eggs and hatch them, safe from any threat, and then, after the chicks lost their down and grew their first real feathers, would come the most beautiful part of the journey: teaching the fledglings to fly in the Bay of Biscay.

Kengah ducked her head to catch her fourth herring, and as a result she didn't hear the squawk of alarm that shattered the air: "Danger to port! Emergency takeoff!"

When Kengah lifted her head from the water, she found herself all alone in the immensity of the ocean.

TWO · A BIG, FAT, BLACK CAT

"I REALLY HATE TO LEAVE YOU BY YOURSELF," the boy said, stroking the big, fat, black cat's back.

Then he returned to the task of putting things in his backpack. He chose a cassette of The Pur, one of his favorites, put it in, thought about it again, and took it out. He couldn't decide whether to put it in the pack or leave it on the table. It was hard to know what to take on vacation and what to leave at home.

The big, fat, black cat sitting in the recessed window, his favorite place, was watching the boy closely.

"Did I put in my swim goggles? Zorba, have you seen my goggles? No. You wouldn't know what they are because you don't like water. You don't know what you're missing. Swimming is one of the most fun sports. Want a treat?" the boy offered, picking up the box of Kitty Yum-Yums.

He shook out a more than generous portion, and the big, fat, black cat began chewing, slowly, to prolong the pleasure. What delicious treats, so crunchy, and so deliciously fishy!

He is a good kid, the cat thought, his mouth filled with crumbs. *What do I mean, a good kid? He's the best!* he corrected himself as he swallowed.

Zorba, the big, fat, black cat, had good reason for his opinion of this boy, who not only spent money from his allowance on delicious treats for Zorba, but always kept the litter box where Zorba relieved himself clean. And he talked to him and taught him important things.

They spent many hours together on the balcony, watching the bustling traffic in the port of Hamburg. Right then, for example, the boy was saying, "You see that ship, Zorba? You know where it's from? It's from Liberia, a very interesting African country founded by people who once were slaves. When I grow up I'm going to be captain of a large sailing ship, and I will sail to Liberia. And you will come with me, Zorba. You will be a good oceangoing cat. I'm sure of it."

Like all the boys around the port, this one too dreamed of voyages to distant countries. The big, fat, black cat listened, purring. He could see himself on board a sailing vessel, cutting through the waves.

Yes. Zorba had great affection for the boy and never forgot that he owed his life to him.

Zorba's debt dated from the day he abandoned the basket that had been home for him and his seven brothers and sisters.

His mother's milk was warm and sweet, but he wanted to try one of those fish heads that people in the market gave to big cats. And he wasn't planning to eat the whole thing. No. His idea was to drag it back to the basket and tell his brothers and sisters, "Enough of this nursing from our poor mother! Don't you see how thin she's getting? Eat this fish, that's what the port cats all eat."

A few days before he left the basket, Zorba's mother had been very serious as she told him, "You are quick on your feet and alert. That's all to the good, but you must be cautious about where you go. I don't want you to get out of the basket. Tomorrow or the next day humans will come and decide your fate, and your brothers' and sisters' as well. I'm sure they will give all of you nice names and you will have all the food you want. You are very lucky to have been born in a port, because in ports humans love and protect cats. The only thing they expect of us is to keep the rats away. Oh, yes, my son. You are very lucky to be a port cat— but you must be careful. There is one thing about you that may mean trouble. Look at your brothers and sisters, son. You see how all of them are gray? And how their fur is striped, like the hide of a tiger? You, on the other hand, were born entirely black, except for that little white tuft under your chin. Some humans believe that black cats bring bad luck. That's why, son, I don't want you to leave the basket."

But Zorba, who at that time was a little coal-black ball of fur, did crawl out of the basket. He wanted to try one of those fish heads. And he also wanted to see a little of the world.

He didn't get very far. As he was trotting toward a fish stall with his tail straight up and quivering, he passed in front of a large bird dozing with its head tilted to one side. It was a very ugly bird with a huge pouch beneath its beak. Suddenly, the little black kitten could not feel the ground beneath his feet and, without any idea of what was happening, he found himself somersaulting through the air. Remembering one of his mother's first teachings, he looked for a place where he could land on all four paws. Instead, what he saw beneath him was the bird, waiting with an open beak. He fell right into its pouch, which was very dark and smelled terrible.

"Let me out! Let me out!" the kitten bawled desperately.

"My . . . it can talk," the bird squawked without opening its beak. "What kind of creature are you?"

"Let me out or I'll scratch," the kitten yowled threateningly.

"I suspect that you're a frog. Are you a frog?" the bird asked, keeping its long bill clamped tightly shut.

"I'm drowning in here, you stupid bird," the little cat cried.

"Yes. You are a frog. A black frog. Curious indeed."

"I am a cat, and am I mad! Let me out or you'll be sorry!" warned little Zorba, looking for somewhere in that dark pouch to sink his claws.

"Do you think I can't tell the difference between a cat and a frog? Cats are furry, quick, and they smell of house slippers. You are a frog. I ate several frogs once, and they weren't bad. But they were green. Say, you wouldn't be a poisonous frog, would you?" the bird croaked, a little worried.

14

"Yes! Yes, I'm a poisonous frog, and besides, I bring bad luck!"

"What a dilemma! Once I swallowed a poisonous sea urchin and nothing happened to me. What a di-*lem*-ma! Shall I swallow you or spit you out?" the bird pondered. Suddenly it stopped squawking and started jumping up and down and flapping its wings. Finally it opened its beak.

Little Zorba, wet with slobber, stuck his head out and jumped to the ground. Then he saw the boy, who had the bird by the neck, shaking it.

"You must be blind, you numbskull pelican! Come on, kitten. You almost ended up in the belly of that ugly old bird," the boy said, and took Zorba up in his arms.

And so had begun the friendship that had lasted five years.

The boy's kiss on his head scattered the cat's memories. He watched his friend settle the pack on his back, walk to the door, and from there said good-bye one more time.

"We won't see each other for four weeks. I'll be thinking of you every day, Zorba. I promise."

"Bye, Zorba!" "Bye!" The boy's two younger brothers shouted and waved their good-byes.

He listened as the two locks turned in the door, then ran to the window that overlooked the street to watch his adoptive family as they drove away.

The big, fat, black cat drew a deep, contented breath. For four whole weeks he would be lord and master of the apartment. A friend of the family would come every day to open a can of cat food and clean Zorba's litter box. Four weeks to laze about in the armchairs, on the beds—or to go out on the balcony, climb to the tile roof, jump from there to the branches of the old chestnut tree, and slide down the trunk to the inner patio, where he liked to meet the other neighborhood cats. He wouldn't be bored. No way.

At least that's what Zorba, the big, fat, black cat, thought, because he had no idea what was to come.

THREE · HAMBURG IN VIEW

KENGAH UNFOLDED HER WINGS to take off, but the approaching wave was too quick. Its force swept her beneath the surface, and when she came back up, the daylight had disappeared. She shook her head again and again, realizing that she had surfaced through the black wave of an oil slick that had nearly blinded her.

Kengah, the gull with feathers once the color of

silver, kept dipping her head deep into the water until a few sparks of light penetrated the thick oil covering her eyes. Sticky blobs the gulls called the black plague glued her wings to her body. She began to kick her feet with the hope that she could swim fast enough to escape from the black tide.

Every muscle cramped with the effort, but at last she came to the edge of the oil slick and paddled into clean water. She blinked and dipped her head until she was able to clear her eyes, but when she looked up at the sky all she saw were a few clouds floating between the sea and the enormous dome of the skies. Her friends from the flock of the Red Sand Lighthouse were already far away, very far away.

That was the rule. She herself had seen other seagulls surprised by the deadly black tides, and though everyone wanted to go back and offer help, they knew that help would be impossible. There was nothing they could do. And so her flock had flown on, respecting the rule that forbids witnessing the death of one's fellow gulls.

With their wings immobilized, stuck fast to their bodies, gulls are easy prey for large fish. Or they may die more slowly, suffocated by the oil that sinks through their feathers and clogs their pores.

That was the fate that awaited Kengah. She hoped

it would be the jaws of a giant fish that would quickly snap her up.

The black stain. As she awaited the end, Kengah cursed all humans. "But not all of them. I should be fair," she squawked weakly.

Often from high above she had watched as large oil tankers took advantage of foggy days along the coast to steam away from land to wash out their tanks. They spilled thousands of liters of a thick, stinking substance into the sea, which then was carried along by the waves. But she also saw how sometimes smaller vessels kept close to the tankers and prevented them from emptying their tanks. Unfortunately, those boats, draped in the colors of the rainbow, didn't always arrive in time to prevent the poisoning of the seas.

Kengah spent the longest hours of her life resting on the waves, wondering with terror whether she was awaiting the most horrible of all deaths. Worse than being eaten by a fish, worse than suffering the torture of suffocation, was dying of hunger.

Desperate at the idea of a slow death, she shook herself and with amazement found that the oil had not glued her wings to her body. Her wings were coated with thick black sludge, but at least she could unfold them.

"I may still have a chance to get out of this, and

who knows, maybe if I can fly high, very high, the sun will melt the oil," Kengah croaked.

She was remembering a story she had heard an old gull from the Frisian Islands tell about a human named Icarus, who, in order to accomplish his dream of flying, had made himself wings of eagle feathers. He had in fact flown . . . high, almost up to the sun, so high that the sun melted the wax he'd used to stick the feathers together, and he fell back to Earth.

Kengah flapped her wings hard, tucked back her feet, lifted about a foot above the waves, and plopped right back down, face first. Before trying again, she dived beneath the waves and moved her wings back and forth. This time when she tried, she rose more than three feet before she fell.

The accursed oil had stuck her tail feathers together so tight that she wasn't able to steer on her ascent. She dived again and pecked at the black gummy substance stuck to her tail. She bore the pain of the feathers she accidentally ripped out until finally she was satisfied that her steering gear was a little less fouled.

On the fifth attempt, Kengah succeeded: She was flying.

She flapped her wings desperately, but the weight of the layer of oil would not let her glide. The minute she rested, she plunged downward. Fortunately, she was a young seagull, and her muscles responded in fine fashion.

She flew higher. Winging, winging, she looked down and could barely make out the fine white line of the coast. She also saw a few ships moving like tiny objects on a blue cloth. She gained altitude, but the hoped-for effect of the sun did not come. Maybe the heat of its rays was too weak, or the layer of oil was too thick.

Kengah knew that her strength could not last much longer, and so, seeking a place to land, she flew inland, following the snaking green line of the Elbe.

The movement of her wings was becoming more leaden, and she was losing strength. Now she was flying lower and lower.

In a desperate attempt to regain some altitude, she closed her eyes and beat her wings with her last ounce of strength. She didn't know how long she kept her eyes closed, but when she opened them she was flying above a tall tower crowned with a golden weather vane.

"Saint Michael's!" she shrieked when she recognized the tower of the Hamburg church.

Her wings refused to stroke another beat.

FOUR • END OF A FLIGHT

THE BIG, FAT, BLACK CAT was taking the sun on his balcony, purring and meditating on how good he felt lying there, belly up, luxuriating in the warm rays of the sun, his four paws folded and his tail straight out.

At the precise moment that he lazily rolled over so the sun could warm his back, he heard the hum of a flying object he couldn't identify, something approaching at great speed. Alert, he leapt up, crouching on all

23

four feet and ready to jump aside to avoid being hit by the seagull that dropped onto the balcony.

It was a very dirty bird. Its whole body was coated with some dark, stinking substance.

Zorba walked toward the gull as she tried to stand up, dragging her wings. "That was not a very elegant landing," he said.

"I'm very sorry. I couldn't help it," the gull admitted.

"*Eeyow!* You look awful. What is that all over you! And you stink something awful!" the cat hissed.

"I was caught in an oil slick. The curse of the seas. I'm going to die," the gull croaked plaintively.

"Die? Don't say that. You're tired and dirty. That's all. Why don't you fly over to the zoo? It isn't too far from here, and there are veterinarians there who can help you," Zorba said.

"I can't. That was my last flight," the gull croaked in an almost inaudible voice, and closed her eyes.

"Don't die on me. Rest a little and you'll see, you'll feel better. Are you hungry? I'll bring you a little of my food, just don't die," Zorba begged, approaching the swooning gull.

Overcoming his disgust, the cat licked the gull's head. The black stuff that covered her tasted as bad as it smelled. As he passed his tongue along her throat, the cat noticed that the bird's breathing was growing weaker and weaker.

"Look, my little friend. I want to help you, but I don't know how. Try to rest while I go find out what you do with a sick gull," Zorba called back, ready to jump to the roof.

As he started off in the direction of the chestnut tree, he heard the gull calling him back.

"Do you want me to leave you a little of my food?" Zorba asked, slightly relieved.

"I am going to lay an egg. With the last strength in my body, I am going to lay an egg. My good cat, anyone can see that you are a fine animal, one with noble sentiments. And for that reason, I am going to ask you to make me three promises. Will you do that for me?" Kengah croaked, slowly paddling her feet in a futile attempt to stand.

Zorba thought the poor gull was delirious, and because she was in such a sorry state, he had no choice but to be generous. "I promise I will do what you ask. But for now, just rest," he mewed with compassion.

"I don't have time to rest. Promise me you won't eat the egg," Kengah croaked, opening her eyes.

"I promise I will not eat the egg," Zorba repeated.

"Promise me that you will look after it until the chick is born," she squawked, holding her neck a little higher.

"I promise I will look after the egg until the chick is born."

"And promise me that you will teach it to fly," Kengah gasped, staring directly into the cat's eyes.

Then Zorba knew that the poor gull was not just delirious, she was totally mad.

"I promise to teach it to fly. And now you rest, I'm going to look for help," Zorba told her, with one leap reaching the tile roof.

Kengah looked toward the sky, thanking all the good winds that had carried her through life, and as she breathed her last sigh, a little blue-speckled white egg rolled free of her oil-soaked body.

FIVE · IN SEARCH OF ADVICE

ZORBA QUICKLY FIRE-POLED down the trunk of
the chestnut tree, raced across the interior patio to
avoid a few roving dogs, went outside, made sure there
was no car coming down the street, crossed, and ran
in the direction of Cuneo, an Italian restaurant in
the port.

Two alley cats sniffing around a garbage pail saw
him go hurrying by.

"Hey, pal! Do you see what I see? Get an eyeful of that good-looking hunk," one yowled.

"Right-o, pal. And so black. Remind you of a lard ball? Nah, more like a ball of tar. Where you going there, tar ball?" the first asked.

Although he was very worried about the seagull, Zorba wasn't about to let the remarks of those two derelicts go by. So he stopped in his tracks and, as the hair rose stiff along his spine, he jumped up on top of the garbage pail.

Slowly he stuck out his front paw, shot out a claw as long and curved as an upholstery needle, and shoved it into the face of one of his would-be tormentors. "You like this? Well, I have nine more. How would you like to have them rake your yellow spine?" he said in a conversational tone.

With that claw right in front of his eyes, the cat swallowed hard before he answered. "I wouldn't, boss. Great day, isn't it? Don't you agree?" The alley cat's eyes never left the claw.

"And you? What do you have to say?" Zorba spit at the second cat.

"Hey, I think it's a nice day too. Great day for a walk, but maybe a little cool."

Having taken care of that matter, Zorba hurried on to the restaurant, where the waiters were setting the tables for the noontime customers. He stopped at the door, meowed three times, and sat down to wait. Within a couple of minutes Secretario, the resident skinny Italian cat, came out. He was nearly whiskerless, with only one long hair on each side of his nose.

"*Scusi*, we ver' sorry, but if you haven' made a reserve, we're not gonna be able serve you. We gotta the full house," Secretario said in his Roman accent. He started to add something more, but Zorba interrupted him.

"I need to have a little chat with the Colonel. It's urgent."

"Urgent! It's always someone with somma last-minute 'mergency. I'll see what can I do, but only because itsa so urgent," Secretario moaned, and went back inside the restaurant.

The Colonel's age was a bit of a mystery. Some said he was as old as the restaurant he called home; others maintained that he was even older. But his age didn't matter, because everyone remembered that as a youth he'd been known as the Nocturnal Colonel, and that he possessed a strange talent for giving advice to cats who had problems. Although the Colonel never actually solved any conflict, his counsel alone was comforting. Both for his age and for his talents, the Colonel was the lead authority among the port cats.

Secretario came back at a trot.

"Follow me. Il Colonnello's gonna see you. Notta the norm . . . " he meowed.

Zorba followed him. Threading through table and chair legs, they headed toward the door of the wine cellar. They bounded down the steps of the narrow stairway and at the bottom found the Colonel, tail like a flagpole, checking the corks of some bottles of champagne. "*Porca miseria!* The rats have chewed the corks of the best champagne in the house. Zorba! *Caro amico!*" the Colonel greeted his dear friend. Just like Secretario, the Colonel liked to show off a little in Italian himself.

"Please forgive me for bothering you just when you're busy at work, but I have a serious problem and I need your advice," Zorba apologized.

"I'm at your service, *caro amico*. Secretario! Serve *al mío amico* here a little of that *lasagna al forno* they gave us this morning," ordered the Colonel.

"But itsa gone! I didn' get so much as a sniff," Secretario complained.

Zorba thanked him, but said he wasn't hungry anyway. Quickly he told the Colonel about the dramatic arrival of the gull, her pitiful condition, and the promises he'd been obliged to make to her. The old cat listened in silence, then mulled over the matter as he

swiped his long whiskers. Finally he yowled, "*Porca miseria!* We must help that poor seagull get in shape to fly again."

"Yes," Zorba said, nodding. "But how?"

"Why don' we go see *il professore*, that Einstein. He'sa know everything," Secretario proposed.

"That is exactly what I was going to suggest. Why did this cat take the very words out of my mouth?" the Colonel protested.

"Yes. Good idea. I will go see Einstein," Zorba agreed.

"We will all go. The problems of one cat of this port are the problems of all the cats of this port," the Colonel declared solemnly.

The three cats left the cellar and, cutting through the labyrinth of interior patios of the row of houses facing the port, hurried toward the temple of the cat called Einstein.

SIX · A STRANGE PLACE

EINSTEIN LIVED in a place rather difficult to describe, because at first view you might think it was a cluttered shop of curious gizmos, a museum of exotic whatchamacallits, a storehouse of mechanical thingamajigs, the most chaotic library in the world, or the laboratory of some brainy inventor of screwball contraptions. But it was none of these things, or rather, it was much more than all these things combined.

The place was called Harry's Port Bazaar, and its owner, Harry, was an old sea dog who, during his fifty years of roaming the seven seas, had devoted himself to collecting every kind of object he could find in the hundreds of ports he had visited.

When old age settled into his bones, Harry had decided to trade his sailor's life for that of a landlubber, and he opened the bazaar that housed the jumble of his collections. He had rented a three-story house on one of the streets in the port, but soon it was too small to exhibit the objects in his bizarre bazaar. Then he rented the house next door; it had two stories and it, too, wasn't big enough. After renting a third house he was able to exhibit the entire conglomeration— arranged, it is true, with a very odd sense of order.

In the three houses, joined by narrow stairways, there were nearly a million objects, among them, some worthy of special note: 7,200 hats with floppy brims that wouldn't be blown away by the wind; 160 wheels from ships dizzy from sailing round and round the world; 245 ship's lights that penetrated the thickest pea soup fogs; 12 engine-order telegraphs battered by the ham hands of irate captains; 256 compasses that never veered from North; 6 wooden life-size elephants; 2 stuffed giraffes posed as if surveying the savanna; 1 stuffed polar bear in whose belly lay the right hand of a Norwegian explorer; 700 fans whose blades, when they whirled, recalled the fresh breezes of dusk in the tropics; 1,200 jute hammocks that guaranteed a perfect night's sleep; 1,300 marionettes from Sumatra that had performed nothing but love stories; 129 slide projectors that showed landscapes in which you could always be happy; 54,000 novels in 47 languages; 2 reproductions of the Eiffel Tower, the first constructed from a half-million pins, the second from 300,000 toothpicks; 3 cannons from English corsairs; 17 anchors from the bottom of the North Sea; 2,000 paintings of sunsets; 17 typewriters that had belonged to famous authors; 128 flannel long johns for men taller than 6 feet; 7 dinner jackets for dwarves; 500 pipes filled with sea foam; 1 astrolabe that stubbornly pointed to the Southern Cross; 7 huge seashells in which you could hear the distant echoes of mythic shipwrecks; 12 kilometers of red silk; 2 submarine hatchways; and other odds and ends too numerous to list.

To visit Harry's bazaar, you had to pay an entrance fee, and once inside you needed a well-developed sense of direction if you didn't want to get lost in the labyrinth of windowless rooms, long corridors, and narrow stairways.

Harry had two pets: Matthew, a chimpanzee who acted as ticket taker and security guard for the old seaman, played checkers with him—of course very badly—drank his beer, and tried to shortchange his customers. The other mascot was Einstein, a small, slim, gray cat that devoted most of his time to studying the thousands of books in Harry's collection.

The Colonel, Secretario, and Zorba trotted into the bazaar with tails raised high. They were sorry not to see Harry behind the ticket desk because the old man always had affectionate words and a piece of sausage for them.

"Just one minute, you fleabags! You're forgetting you have to pay," Matthew yowled.

"Since when does a *gatto* gotta pay?" Secretario protested.

"The sign over the door says, 'Entry fee: two marks.' Nowhere does it say that cats get in gratis. Eight marks or yer out of here," the chimp screeched emphatically.

"*Scusi*, Signor Monkey, but I fear the numbers is not your strong point," Secretario rejoined.

"That's exactly what I was going to say. Once again, you had to rush in ahead of me!" the Colonel complained.

"Blah, blah, blah. Either pay up or get out," Matthew threatened.

Zorba sprang up on the ticket desk and stared into the eyes of the chimp. He stared until Matthew blinked

and his eyes began to water. "All right then, let's say six marks. Any chimp can make a mistake," he squeaked.

Zorba, still staring him down, shot out one claw in his right front paw. "You like this, Matthew? Well I have nine more. Can you imagine all ten dug into that red rump you always have stuck up in the air?" he threatened tranquilly.

"Well, this time I'll look the other way," the chimp agreed, pretending to be calm. "You can go in."

The three cats, tails proudly aloft, disappeared into the maze of corridors.

SEVEN • A PROFESSORLY CAT

"DREADFUL! DREADFUL! Something dreadful has happened," said Einstein, who, like his namesake, knew about everything there is to know.

He was nervously pacing back and forth before an enormous book that lay open on the floor, from time to time holding his head between his front paws. He seemed truly devastated.

"Something . . . it's wrong?" asked Secretario.

"That is precisely what I was going to ask," the Colonel said, and humphed.

"Come on. It can't be that bad," Zorba suggested.

"Not that bad? It's dreadful. Dreadful! Those accursed rats have chewed one entire page out of the atlas. The map of Madagascar has disappeared. It's dreadful," Einstein insisted, tugging at his whiskers.

"Secretario, remind me that I must organize a foray against those devourers of Masacar . . . Masgacar . . . well, you know what I mean," the Colonel meowed.

"Madagascar," Secretario pronounced precisely.

"We'll lend you a hand, Einstein, but right now we're here because we have a big problem, and since you know everything, maybe you can help us," Zorba explained, and immediately told the sad story of the gull to him.

Einstein listened attentively. He nodded as he took in the details, and every time the nervous twitches of his tail expressed too eloquently the emotions Zorba's meows were awakening, he tried to tuck it beneath his hind legs.

". . . and so I left her there, in bad shape, just a while ago . . . ," Zorba concluded.

"Dreadful story! Dreadful! Hmmm, let me think . . . seagull . . . gull . . . oil . . . oil . . . sick gull . . . that's it! We must consult the encyclopedia!" Einstein exclaimed jubilantly.

"The whaaat?" all three cats meowed.

"The en-cy-clo-pe-dia. The book of knowledge. We must look in volumes seven and fifteen, which correspond to the letters G for 'gull' and O for 'oil,'" Einstein stated decisively.

"So show us this enplyco . . . enclididia . . . the thing," the Colonel humphed.

"En-cy-clo-pe-dia," Secretario slowly phrased.

"Which is just what I was going to say!" the Colonel fumed.

Einstein climbed up on an enormous piece of furniture where thick, imposing-looking books sat in a row. When he found the letters G and O on the spines, he clawed those books off the shelf. He jumped down himself and, with a stubby claw worn down from pawing through so many books, he flipped through the pages. The cats watched and kept a respectful silence as they listened to his nearly inaudible mewings.

"Yes, I believe we're on the right path. Very interesting. We're getting close. Here's "guillotine." Mercy, very interesting. Listen to this, my friends: 'a device consisting of a heavy blade held aloft between upright guides and dropped to behead the victim below.' Oh, my. Dreadful," Einstein exclaimed with fascination.

"We're notta interest in what you say about the guillotina. We here about a gull," Secretario interrupted.

"Forgive me. It's just that for me, the encyclopedia is irresistible. Every time I look in its pages I learn something new," Einstein apologized, and leafed forward. "Ah, Gulf Stream, Gulf War, gulfweed . . . gull!"

But what the encyclopedia said about gulls was not very helpful. About the most they learned was that the gull concerning them belonged to the *Argentatus* species, so called because of the silver color of their feathers.

And what they found out about oil was similarly useless in telling them how to help the gull. Worse, they had to put up with a long lecture from Einstein, who insisted on telling them all about the Gulf War of the 1990s.

"Well this is a fine kettle of fish! We're right back where we began," Zorba exclaimed.

"It's dreadful. Dreadful! For the first time ever the encyclopedia has failed me," a disconsolate Einstein admitted.

"And in that enplicosee . . . ecmipodelphia . . . well, you know what I want to say, isn't there any practical advice about how to take out oil stains?" the Colonel wanted to know.

"Inspired! Purely inspired! That's where we should

have begun. I'll get volume nineteen right this minute, letter S for stain remover," Einstein announced giddily as he leaped back onto the bookshelves.

"You see? If you would just stop that odious habit of taking the meows out of my mouth we would know what to do by now," the Colonel scolded the silent Secretario.

On the page where he found the words "stain remover," besides instructions on how to remove stains from marmalade, China ink, blood, and raspberry syrup, they found the formula for removing oil stains.

"'Clean the affected area with a cloth moistened in benzene.' We've got it!" yowled Einstein.

"We don't have anything," Zorba hissed with obvious bad humor. "Where the devil are we going to get benzene?"

"Well if I'm not mistaken, in our cellar we have a large can filled with paintbrushes soaking in benzene. Secretario, you know what you have to do," the Colonel yowled.

"*Scusi*, Signor, but I don't catch," Secretario apologized.

"Very simple: It's easy. You will dip your tail in benzene, and then we will go take care of that poor gull," the Colonel clarified, gazing off in a different direction.

"Ah, no! Notta that! Notta me!" Secretario protested.

"I recall that the menu this afternoon features a double portion of liver and pan gravy," mused the Colonel.

"Dip my tail in *benzina* . . . . *Mamma mia!* Did you say liver and pan gravy?"

Einstein decided to go with them, so all four cats trotted toward the exit. As he watched them go by, the chimpanzee, who had just polished off a beer, favored them with a rumbling belch.

EIGHT · ZORBA BEGINS FULFILLING HIS PROMISES

FOUR CATS jumped from the roof to the balcony, and knew immediately that they were too late. The Colonel, Einstein, and Zorba observed the lifeless body of the gull with respect, while Secretario whipped his tail in the wind to rid it of the smell of benzene.

"I believe we should fold her wings. That is what is done in these cases," the Colonel said sadly.

Overcoming their distaste for the oil-soaked

feathers, they folded the gull's wings close to her body, and in the process they discovered the white egg with blue speckles.

"The egg! She did it! She laid her egg!" Zorba exclaimed.

"You've got yourself in a fine fix now, *caro amico.* A fine fix!" the Colonel warned.

"What am I going to do with an egg?" Zorba asked, increasingly distressed.

"*Bella, bella!* So many things to do with the egg. An omelet, for example," Secretario quickly recommended.

"Oh my, yes. One peep at the encyclopedia will tell us how to prepare a mouthwatering omelet. That subject will be in volume fifteen, letter O, the same as 'oil,'" Einstein assured them.

"Not one more word about an omelet! Zorba promised that poor gull that he would look after her egg and her chick. He gave his word of honor, and the word of one cat of the port is the word of all the cats of the port, so no one touches the egg," the Colonel pronounced solemnly.

"But I don't know how to care for an egg! I've never done this before," Zorba yowled, desperate.

Six eyes turned toward Einstein. Perhaps in his famous en-cy-clo-pe-dia there would be something on *that* subject.

"I must consult volume five, letter E. You may be sure that there we will find everything we need to know about the egg, but for the moment I advise warmth, body warmth, a lot of body warmth." Einstein's tone was preachery and schoolteachery.

"Which means you lie there, but don't make omelet," Secretario advised.

"Precisely what I was going to propose. Zorba, you stay here beside the egg and we will accompany Einstein to see what his enpilope . . . his nincompoopi . . . gad, you know what I'm referring to. We will be back this evening with that information, and then we'll all bury this poor seagull," the Colonel arranged before leaping to the roof.

Einstein and Secretario followed him. Zorba was left on the balcony with the egg and the dead gull. Very carefully he lay down and pawed the egg close to his belly. He felt ridiculous. He thought of the razzing he would get if the two ruffian cats he'd faced down that morning could see him now.

But a promise is a promise, and so, warmed by the sunshine, he fell asleep with the blue-speckled egg next to his big, fat, black stomach.

NINE · A SAD NIGHT

BY THE LIGHT OF THE MOON, Secretario, Einstein, the Colonel, and Zorba dug a hole at the foot of the chestnut tree. Shortly before, taking great care not to be seen by any human, they had dragged the dead gull from the balcony to the interior patio. Quickly they rolled her body into the hole and covered it with dirt. Then the Colonel delivered in a solemn address:

"Brother cats, on this moonlit night we must bid

farewell to the remains of an unfortunate gull whose name we never had a chance to find out. All that we were able to learn about her, thanks to the knowledge of brother Einstein, is that she belonged to the species of *Argentatus* gulls, and that perhaps she came from very far away, there where the river joins the sea. We know very little about her, but the important thing is that she was dying by the time she reached Zorba's balcony—he being one of our own, of course—and that she placed all her faith in him. Zorba promised to care for the egg she laid before she died, and for the chick that will be born from it, and then—most difficult of all, brothers—he promised to teach the chick to fly."

"Fly. Volume six, letter F," they heard Einstein mumble in his whiskers.

"Exactly what Il Colonnello was gonna say. You took the words right outta his mouth," Secretario muttered sarcastically.

". . . promises difficult to carry out," the Colonel continued, ignoring Secretario. "But we know that a cat of the port always lives up to his words. And to help see that that happens, I order brother Zorba to stay with the egg until the chick is born, and brother Einstein to consult his enplicope . . . envelocipede . . . well, those books of his, to see what he can learn about the art of flying. And now we bid farewell to this gull who was a

victim of a disaster caused by humans. Let us stretch our necks toward the moon and caterwaul the song of farewell known to all the cats of the port."

And there at the foot of the old chestnut tree, four cats began to meow-ow-ow their sad litany, and to their yowlings quickly were added those of other neighborhood cats, and then those of the cats on the other side of the river, and to the cats' caterwaulings were joined the howls of the dogs, the mournful peeping of caged canaries and sparrows in their nests, the sad croaking of the frogs, and even the ear-grating screeching of the chimpanzee Matthew.

Lights came on in all the houses of Hamburg, and that night all the town's inhabitants wondered to what they owed the strange melancholy that had suddenly taken hold of the animals.

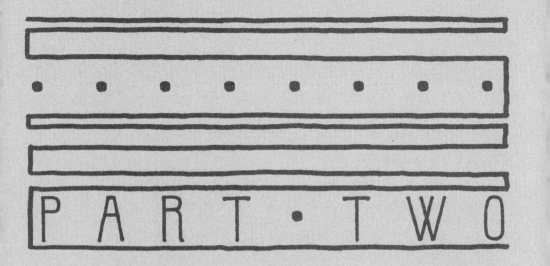

PART · TWO

ONE · BROODY CAT

THE BIG, FAT, BLACK CAT spent many days lying beside the egg, protecting it, rolling it back with gentle, furry paws every time an involuntary movement of his body pushed it an inch or two away. Those were long, uncomfortable days that Zorba sometimes felt were a complete waste, because it felt like he was caring for a lifeless object, a kind of fragile stone, even if it was white with blue speckles.

On one occasion, his body cramped from inactivity—since, in accord with the Colonel's orders, he left the egg only to eat and to visit his litter box—he felt tempted to test whether a little gull chick was growing inside that calcium container. He placed one ear to the egg, then another, but he didn't hear anything. Neither did he have any luck when he tried to see inside the egg as he looked at it against the light. The white shell with the blue speckles was thick and let absolutely no light through.

The Colonel, Secretario, and Einstein visited Zorba every night, and they always examined the egg to see if what the Colonel called "expected progress" was being made, but as soon as they saw that the egg looked exactly the same as it did the first day, they changed the conversation.

Einstein never ceased to lament the fact that his encyclopedia did not reveal the precise length of incubation; the closest fact he was able to extract from his thick books was that it could be between seventeen and thirty days, according to the characteristics of the species to which the mother gull belonged.

Sitting the egg had not been at all easy for the big, fat, black cat. He couldn't forget the morning the friend who came in to look after his needs thought the floor needed to be swept and decided to run the vacuum cleaner.

Every morning during the time the friend was there, Zorba hid the egg among some flowerpots on the balcony in order to devote a few minutes to the nice person who changed the litter in his box and opened his cans of food. He would meow in gratitude and rub against the human's legs, and the human would go away repeating what a nice cat Zorba was. But that morning, after he'd watched the vacuum cleaner roar around the living room and bedrooms, he heard the human say, "And now for the balcony. Dirt seems to really pile up among those flowerpots."

When the friend heard the explosion of a fruit bowl shattering into a thousand pieces, he ran to the kitchen and from the doorway shouted, "What's got into you, Zorba? Look what you've done. Get out of here right now, you crazy cat. That's all we need, for you to get a sliver of glass in your paw."

What an undeserved insult! Zorba slunk from the kitchen with his tail between his legs, pretending to be terribly ashamed, then raced at full speed to the balcony. It wasn't easy to roll the egg from the flowerpots to one of the bedrooms, but he succeeded, and he waited there until the human finished cleaning up and left.

Zorba was drowsing as night fell on day twenty, and that is why he didn't notice that the egg was moving—slowly, but moving, as if it were trying to roll across the floor.

A tickle on his belly woke him. He opened his eyes, and he couldn't help flinching when he saw that a little yellow tip was appearing and disappearing through a crack in the egg.

He steadied the egg between his hind legs and thus was able to watch as the chick pecked and pecked until a hole opened large enough to allow a tiny, damp, white head to emerge.

"Mommy!" the gull chick squawked.

Zorba didn't know how to respond. He knew that his fur was coal black, but he felt as if emotion and embarrassment had turned him pink all over.

TWO • IT ISN'T EASY BEING A MOMMY

"MOMMY! MOMMY!" the chick, now completely out of the egg, squawked again. It was white as milk, and half its body was covered with fine, scraggly, stubby feathers. It tried to take a few steps and fell smack against Zorba's belly.

"Mommy! I'm hungry!" it squawked, pecking at Zorba's fur.

What would he feed it? Einstein hadn't left any

instructions about feeding. He knew that gulls fed on fish, but where was he going to get a piece of fish? Zorba ran to the kitchen and returned rolling an apple.

The chick rose up on its trembling legs and attacked the fruit. The tiny yellow beak tap-tap-tapped against the skin, doubled as if it were rubber and, with the recoil, the chick catapulted backward and fell on its back.

"I'm hungry!" it squawked in a rage. "Mommy! I'm hungry!"

Zorba took the chick into the kitchen and tried to get it to peck a potato, then some of his cat treats— with the family gone he didn't have much to choose from!—regretting that he had emptied his bowl before the chick was hatched. All in vain. The little beak was very soft and it bent as it struck the potato and the treats. Then, at the point of desperation, he remembered that the chick was a bird, and that birds eat insects.

So Zorba hurried out to the balcony and waited patiently for a fly to land within range of his claws. It didn't take long for him to catch one, and he fed it to the hungry baby gull.

The chick pecked at the fly, got it inside its beak and, closing its eyes, swallowed it. "Yummy, Mommy. I want more!" it peeped happily.

Zorba went outside again and started jumping back and forth around the balcony. He had gathered five flies and one spider when, from the roof of the apartment across the patio, came the voices of the two derelict cats he had stared down days before.

"Lookit, pal. Fat boy is doing his rhythmic gymnastics. With a bod like that, no wonder he's a dancer," one yowled.

"Me, I think he's practicing aerobics. And what a divine tub he is. So graceful. What style. Hey, lard ball, are they groomin' you for a beauty contest?" yowled the other.

Both tough cats laughed, safe on the other side of the patio.

Zorba would have been happy to give them the benefit of his razor claws, but they were too far away, so he went back to the hungry chick with his haul of insects.

The chick devoured the five flies but refused to try the spider. Satisfied, it burped and snuggled in tight against Zorba's belly. "I'm sleepy, Mommy," it peeped.

"Listen, I'm sorry about this, but I'm not your mommy," Zorba meowed.

"Of course you're my mommy. And you're a very good mommy," it replied, and closed its eyes.

When the Colonel, Secretario, and Einstein showed up, they found the chick sleeping next to Zorba.

"Congratulations. It's a beautiful little chick. How much does it weigh?" Einstein asked.

"What kind of question is that? I'm not the mother of this chick!" Zorba protested.

"But that is what one always asks in such cases. Don't take it wrong. In fact, it *is* a very pretty chick," said the Colonel.

"Dreadful! Dreadful!" Einstein exclaimed, pressing his front paws to his mouth.

"May we ask what is so dreadful?" the Colonel asked.

"This chick has nothing to eat. It's dreadful. Just dreadful!"

"You're right about that," Zorba agreed. "I had to give it some flies, and I think that before long it's going to want to eat again."

"Secretario, what are you waiting for?" The Colonel thumped a paw impatiently.

"*Scusi*, Signor, but I don' follow."

"Run to the restaurant and bring back a sardine," the Colonel commanded.

"And why me, eh? Why is il Secretario always the errand cat, eh? 'Dip your tail in the *benzina*, Secretario. Run and get a sardina, Secretario.' Why always il Secretario?"

"Because tonight, good sir, we are going to dine on squid Romana," the Colonel replied. "Doesn't that seem like a good reason?"

"My poor tail still stinks of the *benzina* . . . *Mamma mia!* Did you say squid Romana?" Secretario asked before he hustled off.

"Mommy, what are those . . . things?" the chick squawked, pointing its beak at the cats.

"Mommy! It called you Mommy! How dreadfully tender," Einstein blurted out before the look on Zorba's face advised him to think better of it.

"Well, *caro amico,* you have fulfilled the first promise, you are working on the second, and now all that's left is the third," the Colonel declared.

"Right. The easiest. Teach it to fly," Zorba said with irony.

"We shall succeed in that venture. I am consulting the encyclopedia, but research takes time," Einstein reassured him.

"Mommy! I'm hungry!" the chick interrupted.

THREE · DANGER AHEAD

THE COMPLICATIONS BEGAN on the second day after the chick hatched. Zorba had to take drastic measures to prevent the family friend from discovering his protégée. The minute he heard the door open, he turned an empty flowerpot over the chick and sat on it. Fortunately the human didn't come out on the balcony, and couldn't hear the squawks of protest from the kitchen.

The friend, as always, cleaned out Zorba's litter box, opened his can of food and, before he left, looked out the balcony door.

"I hope you're not sick, Zorba, This is the first time you haven't come running when I opened your food. What are you doing sitting on that flowerpot? You'd think you were hiding something. Well, you crazy cat, see you tomorrow."

What if he'd looked under the pot? Just thinking about it turned Zorba's stomach, and he had to run to his box.

There he was, tail high in the air, feeling greatly relieved and thinking about the human's words.

"Crazy cat." That's what he'd called him. "Crazy cat."

Maybe he was right, because the most practical thing would have been to let him see the chick. The friend would have thought that Zorba intended to eat it and would have taken it away to raise until it was grown. But he'd hidden it under a flowerpot. Was he crazy after all?

No. He wasn't. Zorba was rigorously following the honor code of the cats of the port. He had promised the dying gull he would teach the chick to fly, and he would do it. He didn't know how, but he would do it.

Zorba was conscientiously pawing his litter when the alarmed squawking of the chick made him hurry

out to the balcony.

What he saw there froze his blood.

The two derelict cats were lying in front of the chick, tails twitching with excitement, and one of them had a paw on the chick's rear end, holding it down. Fortunately the villains' backs were turned and they didn't see Zorba. Every muscle in his body tensed.

"Who'd a-thought we'd find such a good breakfast, pal. This little chick here looks like the breakfast of kings," one yowled.

"Mommy! Help!" the chick squawked.

"My favoritist part of a bird is the wings. These are pretty scrawny, but the thighs look nice and plump," the other pointed out.

Zorba leapt. In the air he shot out the ten claws of his front paws and landed on the two ruffians, banging their heads against the floor.

They tried to get up, but each time they did, a claw hooked through an ear.

"Mommy! They wanted to eat me!" the chick squawked.

"Eat your kid? No, ma'am. Not us," one yowled, his head plastered to the balcony floor.

"We're vegetarians, ma'am. Strict vegetarians," the other swore.

"I am not a 'ma'am,' you morons," Zorba hissed, jerking

their heads up by the ears so they could see him.

When they recognized him, the two raiding cats felt their hair stand on end.

"Right, pal, that's a good-looking kid you got there. He's gonna make a great cat," the first assured Zorba.

"You can see that a mile away. Yep, a good-looking little cat, all right," the second agreed.

"It's not a cat, stupid. It's a seagull chick," Zorba corrected.

"Yeah, that's what I always tell my buddy here: Everyone should have a little gull," the first exclaimed. "Ain't that right, buddy?"

Zorba decided to end the farce, but first those two cretins were going to take away a souvenir from his claws. He pulled away his front paws, and his claws split an ear on each of those two cowards. Yowling with pain, they beat a fast retreat.

"My mommy is very brave!" the chick shrieked.

Zorba realized that the balcony was not safe, but he couldn't take the chick inside because it would dirty the carpet and ultimately be discovered by the family friend.

"Come on, we're going to take a little walk," Zorba meowed as he delicately picked up the chick between his teeth.

FOUR • DANGER NEVER RESTS

GATHERED IN HARRY'S BAZAAR, the cats decided that the chick could not be left at Zorba's apartment any longer. There were too many risks, and even greater than the threatening presence of the two derelict cats was the human.

"Humans, unfortunately, are unpredictable. Often it's with the best intentions that they cause the greatest damage," the Colonel moralized.

"You're right. Just consider Harry, for example. He's a good man, all heart, and he's fond of the chimp and he knows that Matthew is too fond of his beer. Even so, *blam!* he hands that monkey a bottle every time he gets thirsty," said Einstein. "Now our poor Matthew is an alcoholic. He's beyond shame, and every time he gets drunk he likes to sing off-color songs. Dreadful."

"And when they understand what they do? Jus' think of that nice gull. She died because they crazy, pollutin' the ocean with all their garbages," Secretario added.

After a brief conference, they agreed that Zorba and the chick would live in the bazaar until it learned to fly. Zorba would go back to the apartment every morning so the human didn't get worried, and then would return to look after the chick.

"It's notta be a bad idea to give the *bambino* a name," Secretario suggested.

"Exactly what I was going to propose. I *do* resent your butting in!" the Colonel complained.

"I agree," said Zorba. "It should have a name, but first we have to know if it's a boy or a girl."

He hadn't got that thought out before Einstein had trotted over to consult the volume with the letter S and was flipping through its pages looking for the word "sex."

Unfortunately, the encyclopedia said nothing at all about how to distinguish the sex of a gull chick.

"You have to admit that your encyclopedia hasn't been much help to us," Zorba complained.

"I refuse to accept any criticism of the efficacy of my encyclopedia. All knowledge is contained in these books," Einstein returned, offended.

"What about Seven-aSeas! He's an oceans cat. He's a *gatto* who can tell if our *bambino* is a boy gull or a girl gull," Secretario assured them.

"Exactly what I . . . ! I forbid you to ever . . . !" the Colonel sputtered.

The cats were deep into their discussion, so the chick started wandering around among the dozens of stuffed birds. There were blackbirds, parrots, toucans, peacocks, eagles, and falcons, and it was looking at all of them with terror. Suddenly an animal with red eyes was standing in its way, something that obviously wasn't stuffed.

"Mommy! Help!" the chick shrieked with terror.

The first to reach it was Zorba, and just in time, because at just that instant the rat was stretching its front paws toward the chick's neck.

When it saw Zorba, the rat fled toward a crack in the wall.

"It wanted to eat me!" the little chick squawked,

huddling close to Zorba.

"We didn't think about this danger. I believe we're going to have to have a serious talk with the rats," Zorba said.

"I agree. But don't make too many concessions to those rascals," the Colonel counseled.

Zorba went over to the crack. It was very dark inside, but he could see the red eyes of the rat.

"I want to see your leader," Zorba said decisively.

"I am the leader," he heard from the darkness.

"If you're the leader, then you rats must be lower than cockroaches. Tell your *leader* I want to see him," Zorba insisted.

Zorba heard the rat scrabble away, and heard it slide down a pipe, claws screeching. After a few minutes, Zorba again saw its red eyes in the shadows.

"Our leader will see you. In the cellar of the seashells, behind the pirate's chest, there is a way in," the rat squeaked.

Zorba went down to the seashell room. He looked behind the chest and found a hole in the wall big enough for him to get through. He pawed away the cobwebs and crawled into the world of the rats. It smelled of dankness and filth.

"Follow the drainpipes," squeaked a rat he couldn't see.

He obeyed. The farther he crawled, the more dust and dirt clung to his fur.

He moved through the shadows until he reached a section of the sewer that was dimly lighted by a faint ray of daylight. Zorba guessed he must be under the street, and that the light he saw was sifting through a manhole cover. The place smelled terrible, but it was roomy enough to allow Zorba to stand on all fours. A channel of stinking water cut through the center of the room. Then he saw the leader of the rats: The large, dark gray rodent, its body covered with scars, was running a claw up and down the rings of its tail.

"My, my. Look who's come for a visit. Old fatso," squeaked the leader of the rats.

"Fatso! Fatso!" chorused a dozen rats whose red eyes were the only things Zorba could see.

"I want you to leave the chick alone," he hissed.

"So you cats have a little chick. I knew it. We hear all the dirt down here in these sewers. They say it's a tasty little thing. Very tasty. Hee hee hee," squeaked the rat leader.

"Very tasty! Hee hee hee," chorused the others.

"That chick is under the protection of the cats," Zorba said, not intimidated.

"So you can eat it when it grows up? Without

inviting us? Pretty selfish of you whisker-lickers," the rat accused.

"Selfish! Selfish!" repeated the other rats.

"As you well know, I have liquidated more rats than I have hairs on my body. If anything happens to the chick, your hours are numbered." Zorba's tone was serene.

"Listen, you butterball, have you thought about how you're going to get out of here? We can make mince-cat out of you," the rat threatened.

"Mincecat! Mincecat!" the other rats repeated.

Suddenly Zorba sprang toward the rat leader. He came down on its back, holding its head down with his claws.

"You are this close to losing your eyes. Maybe your gang can make mincecat of me, but you will never see again. Now, will you leave the chick alone?"

"What shocking manners you have. All right," the rat accepted. "No mincecat, no chick. Everything is negotiable in the sewers."

"Then we'll negotiate. What do you want in return for respecting the chick's life?" Zorba asked.

"Free access to the patio. The Colonel ordered our route to the market to be cut off. We want free access to the patio," the rat squeaked.

"Agreed. You may go through the patio, but by night, when the humans won't see you. We cats have to protect our reputations." Zorba let the rat go.

He backed his way out, never taking his eyes from the leader of the rats or from the dozens of red eyes glaring at him with hatred.

FIVE · BOY GULL OR GIRL GULL?

IT WAS THREE DAYS before they could talk with SevenSeas, who was their friend and an oceangoing cat, an authentic oceangoing cat.

SevenSeas was the mascot of *Hannes II*, a powerful barge responsible for keeping the mouth of the Elbe free and clear of silt and refuse. The crew of the *Hannes II* appreciated SevenSeas, a honey-colored cat with blue eyes, whom they considered just another mate in the difficult work of dredging the channel of the river.

On stormy days, SevenSeas wore a yellow oilcloth raincoat tailored to his measure, just like the slickers the crew wore, and he prowled the deck with the frown of sailors accustomed to defying bad weather.

The *Hannes II* had also dredged the harbors of Rotterdam, Antwerp, and Copenhagen, and SevenSeas would tell entertaining stories about those voyages. Oh, yes. He was an authentic oceangoing cat.

"Ahoy!" SevenSeas called out as he entered the bazaar.

The chimpanzee blinked quizzically as he watched the cat approach, rocking from side to side like a sailor and ignoring the importance of Matthew's dignified position as ticket seller for the establishment.

"If you don't know how to say good day, at least pay your entry fee, fleabag," Matthew grunted.

"Dummy to starboard! Did you call me a fleabag? Chatterin' barracuda choppers! Just so you'll know, insects in every port of the world have chomped on this hide. Someday I'll tell you the tale of a certain leech that slapped its suckers into my back and drank my blood till it was so heavy I couldn't carry it. And I'll tell you the one about the fleas on Cacatúa Island that have to feed on seven men to get their fill at cocktail hour. Up anchor, macaque, and don't cut across my bow!" SevenSeas commanded, and kept walking without waiting for the chimp's response.

When he reached the room with the books, he paused at the door to greet the cats gathered there.

"*Moin!*" SevenSeas announced himself. He liked to say "good morning" in the harsh but sweet dialect of Hamburg.

"Capitano! You're here at last. You don't know how much we need you!" the Colonel greeted him.

Quickly, they told SevenSeas the story of the seagull and of Zorba's promises, promises that, they repeated, all of them must keep.

SevenSeas listened with solemn nods of his head.

"Blindin' squid's ink! Terrible things happen at sea. Sometimes I wonder whether humans have gone completely mad, because they're turnin' the ocean into one big garbage dump. I've just come from dredgin' the mouth of the Elbe, and you can't imagine the filth the tides have washed up there. By the shell of the sea turtle! We pulled up barrels of insecticide, old tires, and tons of those accursed plastic bottles humans leave behind on the beaches," SevenSeas reported, boiling with anger.

"Dreadful! Dreadful! If things go on this way, it won't be long before the word 'pollution' will take up all of volume sixteen, letter P," Einstein sighed, scandalized.

"Well, what can this old tar do for your poor bird?" SevenSeas asked.

"You alone, who know the secrets of the sea, can tell us if the chick is a boy gull or a girl gull," the Colonel replied.

They led him to where the chick was happily sleeping off a feast of squid provided by Secretario, who, following the Colonel's orders, had been put in charge of the food detail.

SeavenSeas reached out a paw, examined the chick's head, and then lifted the feathers beginning to sprout on the chick's rear. The chick looked at Zorba with frightened eyes.

"Clackin' crab's claws!" the oceangoing cat proclaimed, amused. "This is a pretty little girl gull who someday is going to lay as many eggs as I have hairs on my tail!"

Zorba licked the little gull's head. He regretted that he hadn't asked the mother what her name was, because if the daughter was destined to continue the flight so tragically interrupted by human indifference, it would be nice if she had her mother's name.

"Considering that the chick had the good fortune to end up under our protection," the Colonel said, "I propose that we call her Lucky."

"Gappin' grouper's gills! Now there's a pretty name

84

for you," SevenSeas cheered. "I recall a beautiful yacht I once saw in the Baltic. That was her name, too, and she was white all over, just like this young gull."

"I know in this heart our *bambina*'s gonna do something great. *Sì*, for sure her name's gonna be in that big book, *numero* twelve, letter L," Secretario added.

Everyone was in favor of the name proposed by the Colonel. The five cats formed a circle around the little gull, rose up on their hind legs and, joining their front paws to make a canopy over the chick, they meowed the baptismal ritual of the cats of the port.

"We salute you, Lucky, dear to all port cats."

"Ahoy! Ahoy! Ahoy!" SevenSeas yowled joyfully.

SIX · LUCKY, TRULY FORTUNATE

LUCKY GREW RAPIDLY, enveloped in the affection of the cats. After a month of living in Harry's bazaar she had grown into a svelte young gull with silky silver feathers.

When tourists visited the bazaar, Lucky followed the Colonel's instructions and sat very still among the stuffed birds, pretending to be one of them. But in the late afternoon, when the bazaar closed and the old sea

dog retired, she waddled with her swaying seabird walk through all the rooms, marveling at the thousands of objects they contained, while Einstein frantically pawed through book after book, looking for the method by which Zorba might teach the fledgling to fly.

"Flying consists of pushing air backward and downward. Aha! Now we have something important," Einstein mused with his nose in a book.

"And why do I have to fly?" Lucky squawked, wings tight against her body.

"Because you are a seagull, and seagulls fly," Einstein replied. "It seems dreadful to me, dreadful! that you don't know that."

"But I don't want to fly. And I don't want to be a seagull, either," Lucky argued. "I want to be a cat, and cats don't fly."

One afternoon she waddled to the entrance of the bazaar, where she had an unpleasant encounter with the chimpanzee.

"I don't want bird droppings around here, you pain-in-the-behind bird!" Matthew screeched.

"Why do you call me that, Mister Monkey?" she asked timidly.

"That's all birds do. Leave droppings everywhere.

And you're a bird," the chimp repeated with authority.

"You're mistaken. I am a cat and very clean," Lucky protested, seeking the simian's sympathy. "I use the same box Einstein uses."

"That's a laugh! What's happened is that that gang of fleabags has convinced you that you're one of them. Look at your body: You have two feet, and cats have four. You have feathers, and cats have fur. And your tail? Eh? Where's your tail? You're as nuts as that cat that spends its life reading and exclaiming, 'Dreadful! Dreadful!' Idiot bird. And do you want to know why your friends are so good to you? Because they're waiting for you to fatten up so they can make a good feast of you. They'll eat you feathers and all!" screeched the chimp.

That afternoon the cats were surprised that the seagull did not show up to eat her favorite dish—the squid that Secretario filched from the restaurant kitchen.

Worried, they went to look for her, and it was Zorba who found her sadly huddled among the stuffed animals. "Aren't you hungry, Lucky? We have squid," Zorba told her.

The gull didn't open her bill.

"Do you feel bad?" Zorba insisted, worried. "Are you sick?"

"Do you want me to eat so I'll get nice and plump?" she asked without looking up.

"No, so you will grow up healthy and strong."

"And when I'm fat, will you invite the rats to eat me up?" she squawked, her eyes filled with tears.

"Where did you get that nonsense?" Zorba yowled angrily.

Tearfully, Lucky recounted everything Matthew had screeched to her. Zorba licked away her tears and soon he heard himself addressing the young seagull as he never had before.

"You are a seagull. The chimpanzee is right about that, but only about that. We all love you, Lucky. And we love you because you *are* a seagull. A beautiful seagull. I haven't contradicted you when I've heard you squawk that you're a cat, because it flatters us that you want to be like us, but you're different and we're happy that you're different. We weren't able to help your mother, but we can help you. We've protected you from the moment you pecked your way out of your shell. We've given you all our affection without ever thinking of making a cat out of you. We love you as a gull. We feel that you love us too, that we're your friends, your family, and we want you to know that with you we've learned something that makes us very proud: We've learned to appreciate and respect and love someone who's different from us. It's very easy to accept and love those who are like us, but to love someone different is very hard, and you have helped us do that. You are a seagull, and you must follow your destiny as a seagull. You must fly. When you do learn, Lucky, I promise you that you'll be happy, and then your feelings toward us and ours for you will be even deeper and more beautiful because it will be affection between totally different creatures."

"I'm afraid to fly," Lucky squawked, standing up.

"When it happens, I will be with you," Zorba meowed, licking Lucky's head. "I promised your mother."

The young gull and the big, fat, black cat began walking back—he licking her head tenderly, and she extending one of her wings across his back.

SEVEN • LEARNING TO FLY

"**BEFORE WE START**, we need to review the technical aspects one last time," Einstein began.

From the top of the bookshelves, the Colonel, Secretario, Zorba, and SevenSeas were attentively observing what was going on below. Lucky was standing at the end of a corridor that had been designated the runway, and at the other end was Einstein, bent over volume twelve, letter L of the encyclopedia. It lay open to one of the pages devoted to Leonardo da Vinci, where there was an illustration of a strange contraption the great Italian master had called a "flying machine."

"If you please," directed Einstein. "First we must confirm the stability of points of support A and B."

"Testing points of support A and B," Lucky repeated, jumping first on her left foot and then on the right.

"Perfect. Now we will test the extension of points C and D," instructed Einstein, who felt as important as an engineer for NASA.

"Testing extension of points C and D," obeyed Lucky, extending her wings.

"Perfect!" Einstein said approvingly. "Let us repeat that once more."

"Whistlin' walrus whiskers!" yowled SeavenSeas. "Just let the girl fly!"

"Let me remind you that I am the technician responsible for this flight!" Einstein rejoined. "Every aspect must be fully checked or else the consequences could be dreadful for Lucky. Dreadful!"

"*Naturalmente*. He know what he do," Secretario seconded.

"That is *exactly* what I was going to say," steamed the Colonel.

* * *

During the last week two events had happened to make the cats realize the gull truly wanted to fly, even though she disguised her feelings very well.

The first had occurred one afternoon when Lucky went with the cats to take the sun on the roof of Harry's bazaar. After enjoying the rays for an hour or so, they saw three gulls flying high, high overhead.

They looked beautiful, majestic, outlined against the blue of the sky. At times they seemed to be frozen in space, simply floating on air with extended wings, but then with one slight movement they thrust forward with a grace and elegance that wakened envy and made the watchers want to be up there with them. Something made the cats turn from the sky to look at Lucky. The young seagull was watching the flight of her fellow gulls, and without realizing she had stretched out her wings.

"Look at that. She wants to fly," the Colonel whispered.

"Yes, it's time for her to learn," Zorba agreed. "She's a big, strong gull."

"Lucky! *Volare!* Try!" Secretario called out to her.

But when she heard the encouragements of her friends, Lucky silently folded her wings and moved closer to them. She lay down beside Zorba and began to click her bill, pretending she was purring.

The second thing had happened the following day as the cats were listening to one of SevenSeas's stories.

"... and as I was telling you, the waves were so high, we couldn't sight the coast, and worst of all—great grinnin' dolphins—our compass was busted. Five days and five nights we were battered by the storm, not knowin' whether we were sailing toward land or out to sea. Then, just when we thought everything was lost, the lookout saw a flock of gulls. We were one happy crew, my friends. We changed course in the direction the gulls were flyin', and that was how we made land. Chatterin' barracuda choppers! Those gulls saved our lives! If we hadn't seen them, old SevenSeas wouldn't be here tellin' this tale to you landlubbers."

Lucky, who always followed the oceangoing cat's stories with great attention, had listened to this one wide-eyed. "You mean seagulls fly during storms?" she asked.

"Why, gulls are the strongest birds in the universe," SevenSeas assured her. "No bird knows more about flyin' than a gull."

The tales of the oceangoing cat struck deep in Lucky's heart. She thumped the floor with her feet, and her bill clicked nervously.

"So, then, Miss Lucky, you think you want to fly?" Zorba asked.

Lucky looked at them, one by one, before she

answered: "Yes! Please, teach me to fly!"

The cats yowled their joy and immediately put paws to the task. They had been waiting a long time for this moment. With the patience characteristic of cats, they had waited for the young gull herself to communicate her wish to fly, because ancestral wisdom had taught them that flying is a very personal decision. Happiest of all was Einstein, who by now had ferreted out the basics of flight in volume twelve, letter L of the encyclopedia, and for that reason had assumed responsibility for directing operations.

"Ready for takeoff!" Einstein announced.

"Ready for takeoff!" Lucky echoed.

"Begin your taxi down the runway by pushing back with points of support A and B."

Lucky began to move forward, but slowly, as if she were rolling on rusty wheels.

"More speed," Einstein urged.

The young gull waddled a little faster.

"Now, extend points C and D."

Lucky extended her wings as she moved forward.

"Now! Lift point E!" ordered Einstein.

Lucky elevated her tail feathers.

"And now! Move points C and D up and down to

push air downward, and at the same time lift points *A* and *B!*"

Lucky flapped her wings, picked up her feet, rose a few inches, and immediately dropped like lead.

The cats leaped down from the bookshelves and ran to her. They found her with tear-filled eyes.

"I'm a failure! I'm a failure!" she repeated, disconsolate.

"No one ever flies on the first try, you will learn. I promise you," Zorba meowed, licking her head.

Einstein kept working at detecting the problem, going over Leonardo's flying machine again and again.

EIGHT · THE CATS DECIDE TO BREAK THE TABOO

SEVENTEEN TIMES Lucky attempted to fly, and seventeen times she ended up on the floor after rising only a few inches.

Einstein, thinner even than usual, had yanked out his whiskers after the first twelve failures, and with a trembling voice tried to apologize.

"I do not understand. I have conscientiously checked the theory of flight. I have compared

Leonardo's instructions with everything in the section devoted to aerodynamics, volume one, letter A of the encyclopedia, and I still can't find the problem. It's dreadful. Dreadful!"

The cats accepted his explanations and were centering all their attention on Lucky, who, with every failed attempt, became more sad and melancholy.

Following the most recent failure, the Colonel had decided to suspend the experiments, for his experience told him that the gull was beginning to lose confidence in herself, and that could be very dangerous if she truly hoped to fly.

"Maybe she'sa not able," Secretario suggested. "Maybe she'sa lived too long with us and has lost the how to fly."

"If one follows the technical instructions and respects the laws of aerodynamics, it is possible to fly. Never forget that it is all here in the encyclopedia," Einstein pointed out.

"Sufferin' stingrays!" exclaimed SevenSeas. "She's a seagull, and seagulls fly!"

"She has to fly. I promised her mother and I promised her. She has to fly," Zorba repeated.

"And each of us is responsible for keeping that promise," the Colonel reminded them.

"We have to admit that we don't know how to teach

her to fly; we must look for help beyond the cat world,"
Zorba proposed.

"You're a straight-talker, *caro amico*. Where do you
want to go?" the Colonel asked seriously.

"I seek your authorization to break the sacred taboo
for the first and last time in my life," Zorba requested,
staring deep into his companions' eyes.

"Break the taboo!" the cats yowled in unison, claws
exposed and hair bristling along their backs.

"To speak the language of humans is taboo" had
always been the code of the cat, and not because cats
hadn't been interested in communicating with
humans. The risk lay in how the humans would
respond. What would they do with a talking cat?
Almost surely they would cage it and put it through all
manner of stupid tests, because in general, humans
are incapable of accepting that a creature unlike them
could understand them and try to be understood. Cats
were aware, of course, of the sad fate of the dolphins,
who had displayed their intelligence to humans who
had in turn condemned the dolphins to acting like
clowns in aquatic spectacles. And they also knew about
the humiliations to which humans subject any animal
that shows itself to be intelligent and receptive to
them. Lions, for example, those big cats forced to live
behind bars. They suffer the shame of letting some

idiot stick his head in their jaws. And parrots, they have to live in cages, imitating humans' stupid chatter over and over. That was why meowing in the tongue of the humans presented a very grave risk for cats.

"You stay here with Lucky. We will retire to debate your request," the Colonel ordered.

The meeting of the cats, conducted behind closed doors, lasted a long time. Long hours during which Zorba lay close beside the gull, who couldn't hide her dejection at not being able to fly.

It was night before they finished. Zorba padded toward them to learn their decision.

"The cats of the port authorize you to break the taboo—this one time only! You will speak with a single human, but first we must decide which among them it will be," the Colonel declared solemnly.

NINE • CHOOSING THE HUMAN

IT WASN'T EASY to decide which human Zorba would consult. The cats made a list of all the humans they knew, and started discarding them one by one.

"René, the chef at the restaurant, is undoubtedly a fair and generous human. He always sets aside a portion of his special dishes for us, and Secretario and I devour them with pleasure. But the only things our good René understands are spices and saucepans; he would not be much help in this case," the Colonel affirmed.

"Harry, too, is a good person. He's understanding and friendly with everyone, even that Matthew, whom he forgives for dreadful behavior, dreadful! Like drenching himself with patchouli, which smells dreadful. Dreadful! But although Harry may know a lot about the sea and about sailing, when it comes to flying, he knows zero," Einstein contributed.

"Carlo, the maître d' at *il ristorante*, says that I'ma belong to him, and I let him believe it 'cause he's good fellow. I'm sad to tell, though, that he knows the soccer, the basketball, the volleyball, the horse race, the box, and many more, but never he say nothin' 'bout the flying," Secretario reported.

"My captain's a very good man, so soft-hearted that in his last fight in a bar in Antwerp he took on twelve guys who had insulted him and left only *half* of them out of commission. But great clamorin' clamshells, he gets dizzy just climbin' up on a chair. I don't see how he can help us," SevenSeas added decisively.

"The boy at my house would understand me," Zorba said. "But he's on vacation, and, anyway, what could a little boy know about flying?"

"*Porca miseria!* That's the end of our list," the Colonel growled.

"No. There is still one human who isn't on our list," Zorba countered. "The one who lives with Angelina."

Angelina was a pretty black-and-white cat who spent long hours taking her ease among the flower-pots on a terrace. All the tomcats of the port paraded slowly past her, showing off the suppleness of their bodies, the gleam of their carefully groomed coats, the length of their whiskers, the elegance of their high-rigged tails, all to impress her, but Angelina was indifferent to them all; she accepted affection only from her human, who sat on the terrace hour after hour at a typewriter.

He was a strange human, who sometimes laughed after he read what he'd just written and other times folded up the sheets of paper without reading them. His terrace was always softly flooded with soft and melancholy music that made Angelina drowsy and drew deep sighs from the tomcats passing by.

"Angelina's human? Why him?" the Colonel asked.

"I don't know. But I feel I can trust that human," Zorba confessed. "I've heard him read what he's written. Beautiful words that make you happy or make you sad, but they always please you and make you want to hear more."

"A poet! What that human does is called poetry. Volume seventeen, letter P, in the encyclopedia,"

Einstein assured them.

"Why you think this Angelina's human knows the flying?" Secretario wanted to know.

"Maybe he doesn't know how to fly with bird's wings, but when I've listened to him it's always made me feel he's flying with his words," Zorba replied.

"All who agree that Zorba should go to see Angelina's human, please raise your right paw," the Colonel proclaimed.

And that was how they authorized Zorba to consult with the poet.

TEN • A FEMALE CAT, A MALE CAT, AND A POET

ZORBA SET OUT across the roof tiles toward the terrace of the chosen human. When he saw Angelina reclining among the flowerpots, he stared and sighed before he meowed. "Angelina, don't be alarmed. I'm up here."

"What do you want? Who are you?" the beauty asked, startled.

"Don't leave, please. My name is Zorba, and I live

near here. I need your help. May I come down?"

Angelina nodded. Zorba leapt down to the terrace and sat on his haunches. Angelina came over to sniff him.

"You smell of books, of damp, of old clothes, of a bird, and of dust, but your coat is clean," Angelina approved.

"Those are the smells of Harry's bazaar. Don't be surprised if I smell of chimpanzee as well," he warned her.

Soft music wafted out onto the terrace.

"What pretty music."

"Vivaldi. *The Four Seasons*. What do you want of me?" Angelina queried.

"I want you to invite me inside and introduce me to your human," Zorba answered.

"Impossible. He's working, and no one, not even me, is supposed to bother him," the cat replied.

"Please, this is a very urgent matter. I ask you in the name of all the cats of the port," Zorba pleaded.

"Why do you want to see him?" Angelina asked, slightly suspicious.

"I need to speak with him," Zorba insisted.

"That's taboo!" Angelina yowled as the hair stood up on her back. "Go away!"

"No. And if you won't invite me in . . . well, have him come out here! Do you like rock music, beautiful?"

Indoors, the human was typing. He was feeling happy because he was on the verge of finishing a poem and the lines were flowing with amazing ease. Suddenly from the terrace he heard the yowling of a cat that wasn't Angelina. The caterwauling was badly out of tune, but it did seem to have a certain beat. Half annoyed, half intrigued, he went out on the terrace and had to rub his eyes to believe what he was seeing.

Angelina had her front paws over her ears; in front of her was a big, fat, black cat sitting on the base of his spine and leaning back against a flowerpot. He was holding his tail with a front paw as if it were a bass fiddle, and with the other paw he was pretending to pluck its strings, all the time yowling nerve-curdling meows.

Once over his surprise, the human couldn't help but laugh, and when he doubled over, holding his stomach from laughing so hard, Zorba took advantage of the moment to slip inside the house.

When the human, still weak with laughter, went back inside, he found the big, fat, black cat sitting in a chair.

"That was some concert! You're a very original Don Juan, but I'm afraid that Angelina doesn't like your music. It was a godawful concert!" the human said.

"I know I'm a terrible singer. No one's perfect," Zorba replied in the language of the humans.

The human opened his mouth, clapped one hand to his head, and fell back against the wall.

"You're . . . you're . . . talking," the human exclaimed.

"You're talking too, and I'm not surprised. Please, be calm," said Zorba.

"A . . . a c-c-cat . . . that talks!" Now the human collapsed onto the sofa.

"I don't talk, I meow, but in your language. I know how to meow in many languages," Zorba said.

The human covered his eyes with his hands and repeated, "I'm just tired, I'm just tired." When he took his hands away, the big, fat, black cat was still on the chair.

"I'm hallucinating. You're just an hallucination, right?" the human asked.

"No, I'm a real cat sitting here talking with you," Zorba assured him. "The cats of the port have chosen you, among many humans, to confide a great problem to. We're hoping you will help us. You're not crazy. I'm real."

"You say you speak in many languages?" the human asked, still doubting.

"I suppose you want proof. Well, go ahead, try me."

"*Buon giorno*," the human said.

"It's late in the day for that. *Buona sera* would be better," Zorba corrected.

"*Kalimera*," the human insisted in Greek.

"*Kalispera*, I told you that it's late," Zorba corrected a second time.

"*Dobroye utro!*" the human shouted in Russian.

"*Dobry den*. Do you believe me now?" Zorba asked.

"Yes. And even if this is a dream, so what? I like it and I want to keep dreaming it," the human replied.

"Good, then let's get down to it," Zorba proposed.

The human nodded, but he asked Zorba to respect the ritual of humans' conversations. He served Zorba a plate of milk, and he sat down on the sofa with a glass of cognac in his hand.

"Speak on, cat," said the human, and so Zorba told him the story of the dying gull, the egg, little Lucky, and the fruitless efforts of the cats to teach her to fly.

"Can you help us?" Zorba asked when he had finished his cat tale.

"I think I can. And this very night," the human responded.

"This very night? Are you sure?"

"Look out the window, cat. Look at the sky. What do you see?" asked the human.

"Clouds. Black clouds. A storm's on the way, and it will rain very soon," Zorba observed.

"Well, that's why tonight," said the human.

"I don't understand. I'm sorry, but I don't understand."

The human went to his desk, took out a book, and searched through the pages. "Listen, cat. I'm going to read you something by a poet named Bernardo Atxaga. A few lines from a poem entitled 'Gulls.'"

'But their small hearts
— the hearts of all aerialists —
long for nothing
as much as for the wild rain
that almost always brings wind,
that almost always brings sun.'

"I get it now. I knew you'd be able to help us," said Zorba, leaping from the chair.

They agreed to meet at midnight outside the door of the bazaar, and the big, fat, black cat loped off to inform his companions.

ELEVEN • FLIGHT

A HEAVY RAIN was falling over Hamburg, and the smell of wet earth was rising from the gardens. The asphalt streets were gleaming, and the neon signs were reflected, distorted, on wet sidewalks. A man in a raincoat was walking down a deserted street toward Harry's Port Bazaar.

"No way!" screeched the chimpanzee. "I don't care if you sink *fifty* claws in my rear end, I will not open the door for you!"

"But no one wants to hurt you. We're asking a favor, that's all," Zorba pleaded.

"The hours we're open are from nine in the morning to six in the evening. That's the rule, and it has to be respected," shrieked Matthew.

"Gelatinous jellyfish! Can't you be a decent fellow just once in your life, macaque?" yowled SevenSeas.

"Please, Mister Monkey," Lucky squawked pleadingly.

"Im-possible! The rules forbid me from reaching out a paw to unlock the lock that you fleabags, having no fingers, cannot open," Matthew screeched scornfully.

"You are a dreadful primate! Dreadful," muttered Einstein.

"There's a human out there lookin' at his watch," cried Secretario, who was peeking through a window.

"It's the poet! There is no time to lose!" said Zorba, charging full speed toward the window.

As the bells in the church of Saint Michael's began to peal midnight, the human was startled to hear the sound of breaking glass. The big, fat, black cat dropped to the street in the midst of a shower of splinters, but he kept his feet, ignoring the cuts on his head, and jumped back up to the window he'd just blasted through.

The human got there at the precise moment that

several cats were lifting a gull up toward the windowsill. Behind the cats, a chimp's hands were fluttering across his face, trying to cover his eyes, his ears, and his mouth all at the same time.

"Take her. Don't let her get cut by the glass," Zorba warned.

"Come here, both of you," said the human, taking cat and gull in his arms.

The human hurried away from the bazaar window. Beneath his raincoat he carried a big, fat, black cat and a gull with silver feathers.

"Lowlifes! Bandits! You'll pay for this!" screeched the chimpanzee.

"It's your deserves! And you know what Harry's gonna think tomorrow? That you smashed his window," said Secretario.

"Bully for you," sputtered the Colonel. "For once you hit the mark when you beat me to the punch."

"Fleet flying fish! To the rooftop, mates. We are going to see our Lucky fly," meowed SevenSeas.

The big, fat, black cat and the gull were very comfortable beneath the coat, bathed in the warmth of the human striding along with firm, quick steps. They could feel their three hearts beating at different rhythms, but with the same intensity.

"Did you hurt yourself, cat?" the human asked

when he saw the bloodstains on the lapels of his rain-coat.

"It isn't important. Where are we going?" asked Zorba.

"Do you understand the human?" Lucky squawked.

"Yes. He is a good person who is going to help you fly," Zorba assured her.

"Do you understand the gull?" the human asked.

"Tell me where we are going," Zorba persisted.

"We're not going, we're there," the human replied.

Zorba stuck out his head. They had stopped before a tall building. He looked up and recognized the tower of Saint Michael's, illuminated by several spotlights. The beams were focused on the slim structure covered with sheets of copper on which time, rain, and wind had left a green patina.

"The doors look closed," wailed Zorba.

"Not all of them," said the human. "I often come here on stormy nights to smoke and think in solitude. I know a way in."

They walked around a corner and went through a small side door that the human opened with the help of a knife blade. He took a flashlight from one pocket and, guided by its faint beam, they began to climb a spiral staircase that seemed never to end.

"I'm afraid," Lucky squawked.

"But you want to fly, don't you?" meowed Zorba.

From the bell tower of Saint Michael's they could see the whole city. Rain enveloped the television tower, and in the port the cranes looked like animals at rest.

Zorba pointed toward a lighted building. "Look, there's Harry's bazaar. That's where our friends are," said Zorba.

"I'm afraid, Mommy!" squawked Lucky.

Zorba leaped up on the railing that encircled the bell tower. Below, automobiles were crawling along like insects with glittering eyes. The human took the gull in his hands.

"No! I'm afraid! Zorba! Zorba!" Lucky cried, pecking at the human's hands.

"Wait! Set her down on the railing," Zorba said to the human.

"I wasn't planning to drop her," said the human.

"You are going to fly, Lucky. Take a breath. Feel the rain. That's water. In your lifetime you will have many reasons to be happy. One of them is called water, another is called wind, another sun, and it always comes as a reward after the rain. Feel the rain. Open your wings," Zorba said patiently.

The gull stretched her wings. The spotlights bathed her with light, and the rain spattered her feathers with pearls. The human and the cat watched her lift her head, with her eyes closed.

"Rain. Water. I like them," she said.

"You are going to fly," Zorba said again.

"I love you, Zorba. You are the best cat in the world," Lucky said, moving toward the edge of the banister railing.

"You are going to fly. The whole sky will be yours."

"I will never forget you. Or the other cats." Lucky was teetering with half her feet off the railing, because, as Atxaga's poem said, she had the heart of an aerialist.

"Fly!" Zorba cried, reaching out with one paw and giving her the lightest of taps.

Lucky disappeared from view, and the human and the cat feared the worst. She had fallen like a stone. Holding their breath, they leaned over the railing, and then they saw her, beating her wings, flying over the parking lot, and then they followed her flight upward, up higher than the golden weather vane that crowned the singular beauty of Saint Michael's.

Lucky was flying alone in the night over Hamburg. She flew away, rapidly beating her wings, until she rose above the cranes in the port and above the masts of the ships, and then she returned, gliding, circling

again and again around the bell tower of the church.

"I'm flying! Zorba! I can fly!" she squawked ecstatically from the vastness of the gray skies.

The human stroked the cat's back. "Well, cat, we did it," he said, sighing.

Zorba seemed to reflect for a moment. "Yes. At the edge of the void she understood the most important thing of all," Zorba said.

"Oh, yes? And what was that?" the human asked.

"That only those who dare may fly."

"I suppose I'm just in the way now. I'll wait below," the human said, and left.

Zorba sat there watching the gull until he didn't know whether it was raindrops or tears that were filling the yellow eyes of a big, fat, black cat . . . a good cat, a noble cat, a cat of the port.

Laufenburg, The Black Forest, 1996

This book was designed and art directed by David Saylor.
Chris Sheban's artwork for the jacket was created using
watercolor and pencil on Arches watercolor paper, and the
artwork for the interior was created using charcoal pencil
and pastel on Strathmore drawing paper. The text was set
in 12-point Bancroft Book, a typeface designed by American
type designer Robby Woodard and released by GarageFonts
in November 2000. The book was printed on 70-pound
acid-free trade book cream paper and bound at Berryville
Graphics in the United States of America. The manufactur-
ing was supervised by Angela Biola.